A NOTE TO PARENTS

Disney's **First Readers Level 3** books were developed for children who have mastered many basic reading skills and are on the road to becoming competent and confident readers.

Disney's First Readers Level 3 books have more fully developed plots, introduce harder words, and use more complex sentence and paragraph structures than Level 2 books.

Reading is the single most important way a young person learns to enjoy reading. Give your child opportunities to read many different types of literature. Make books, magazines, and writing materials available to your child. Books that are of special interest to your child will motivate more reading and provide more enjoyment. Here are some additional tips to help you spend quality reading time with your child:

★ Promote thinking skills. Ask if your child liked the story or not and why. This is one of the best ways to learn if your child understood what he or she has read.

★ Continue to read aloud. No matter how old the child may be, or how proficient a reader, hearing a delightful story read aloud is still exciting and a very important part of becoming a more fluent reader.

★ Read together on a regular basis, and encourage your child to read to you often. Be a good teacher by being a good listener and audience!

★ Praise all reading efforts, no matter how small.

★ Try out the After-Reading Fun activities at the end of each book to enhance the skills your child has already learned.

Remember that early-reading experiences that you share with your child can help him or her to become a confident and successful reader later on!

— Patricia Koppman
Past President
International Reading Association

Pencils by Karen Rosenfield

First published by Disney Press, New York, New York.
This edition published by Scholastic Inc.,
90 Old Sherman Turnpike, Danbury, Connecticut 06816
by arrangement with Disney Licensed Publishing.

SCHOLASTIC and associated logos are trademarks of Scholastic Inc.

ISBN 0-7172-6465-3

Printed in the U.S.A.

GENIE SCHOOL

by K. A. Alistir
Illustrated by Christian Monte
and Adam Devaney

Disney's First Readers — Level 3
A Story from Disney's *Aladdin*

⭐⭐⭐

SCHOLASTIC INC.

New York Toronto London Auckland Sydney
Mexico City New Delhi Hong Kong Buenos Aires

It was a beautiful day in Agrabah. High on a hill above the town, the palace gleamed in the sun.

"Last one to the palace . . ." Aladdin began.

"... is a rotten egg!" finished Princess Jasmine.

Suddenly, the air began to stir. In a blur of blue, a smiling genie took shape.

"Did someone say eggs?" asked
the Genie. He held out a plate of
scrambled eggs.

"Thanks, Genie," Aladdin replied.
"How did you know I skipped breakfast?"

Before Aladdin could take a bite, a furry hand grabbed the plate of eggs.

"Abu skipped breakfast, too," Jasmine laughed, pointing to Aladdin's pet monkey.

Abu handed Aladdin the empty plate. "Thanks, Abu," Aladdin said. "You're more fun than a barrel of monkeys."

"You said it, Al," the Genie added. Then, Genie snapped his fingers and said, "Ka-zam!" Suddenly, a big wooden barrel appeared out of nowhere.

"No offense, Abu," the Genie said, as
a dozen monkeys popped out of the
barrel and began to sing and dance.

At the end of their song, the
monkeys took a bow. Then, they
climbed back into the barrel.
In a flash, the barrel disappeared.

"Wow!" Aladdin gasped. "What a great trick!"

"Where did you learn to do it?" asked Jasmine.

"In genie school, of course," the Genie said.

"Genie school?" Aladdin repeated. "Is there really such a place?"

"You bet," the Genie said. "Just close your eyes and you'll see."

Aladdin and Jasmine closed their eyes. Abu covered his eyes. But he still peeked.

"Ka-zam!" the Genie said.

In a snap, Aladdin and Jasmine were sitting in a very strange classroom. The room was filled with little genies.

The little genies looked just like the big genie—except for the blue part. There were yellow genies, red genies, purple genies, and even a teeny-weeny green genie.

Appearing &

The Genie took his place at the front of the room. He floated a few feet off the ground.

"Good morning, class," said the Genie. "Today we are going to review yesterday's lesson. Appearing and dis—"

But before the Genie could say "disappearing," all the yellow genies, red genies, purple genies, and even the teeny-weeny green genie were gone!

Disappearing

A moment later, they were
back in their seats.
"Bravo! Bravo!" the Genie
said proudly.

"I guess he wasn't kidding about genie school," Jasmine said to Aladdin. The Genie floated over their heads. "Hey, would I kid you?" he asked.

Before Aladdin and Jasmine could answer, a nanny goat and her three kids trotted in from nowhere. They erased the chalkboard with their tails. When it was clean, the Genie made the goats disappear.

"Now, let's do some mathematics," said the Genie.

"Math!" groaned the teeny-weeny green genie. "Who needs math?"

"Everyone," the Genie said. "Think about it. We give out three wishes. No ifs, ands, or buts."

3 Wishes
~3 Wishes
=? Wishes

"If you don't learn your numbers, who knows how many wishes you might grant? Your work would never get done. Now, count along with me," the Genie said.

When their math lesson was over, the little genies had some milk and cookies.

"The Genie is a very good teacher," Aladdin said. "But I also know a few tricks."

"Really?" Jasmine cried. "Show me."

"I just made three delicious cookies disappear," grinned Aladdin. He bowed.

"That's your trick?" Jasmine asked.

"Watch this. I can grow a mustache." Jasmine gulped down a glass of milk.

"Ka-zam!" she said.

After all the genies gobbled the last
of the cookies and swallowed the last of
the milk, it was time for a nap.

The Genie dimmed the lights. All the
genies—the yellow ones, red ones,
purple ones, and the teeny-weeny green
genie—disappeared into their lamps.

After a short snooze, the genies were ready to learn their ABCs.

"A is for apple," began a red genie.
He snapped his fingers and an apple
appeared on his desk.

"B is for banana," a yellow genie said next. She snapped her fingers and a banana appeared on her desk.

"This looks easy," Aladdin told Jasmine. "C is for chocolate candy," he said, snapping his fingers. One snap. Two snaps. Three snaps.

Nothing happened.

Aladdin snapped three more times.
Nothing.

All the little genies giggled. The
teeny-weeny green genie laughed
so hard, he fell off his chair.

"I guess it's not as easy as it looks,"
Aladdin said.

"Actually, Al," the Genie said, floating overhead, "it's as easy as pie."

He snapped his fingers and a gooey chocolate-cream pie appeared on Aladdin's desk.

Aladdin and Jasmine dipped their forks into the pie.

"Mmmm," Jasmine said. "Delicious."

"C is for creamy," said Aladdin.

Abu scooped out a big piece of pie for himself.

At three o'clock,
 the bell rang.
"School's out!"
 cried the Genie.

All the genies . . .

. . . floated away

. . . on their

. . . magic carpets!

"How will we get home?"
asked Aladdin. "We don't have
a magic carpet."
"Ka-zam!" cried the Genie.

Suddenly, Aladdin and Jasmine were back in Agrabah. Abu was with them, too.

"Let's try those genie school tricks," Aladdin said. "B is for banana!"

Aladdin snapped his fingers. Nothing.

In a whirl of blue, the Genie appeared.
He handed Abu a bunch of bananas.
"But, why can't I do that, Genie?"
said Aladdin. "I went to genie school."

"True, Al, my pal," said the Genie.
"But all that appearing and
disappearing stuff is for genies only."
And to make his point . . .

. . . the Genie disappeared!

AFTER-READING FUN

Enhance the reading experience with follow-up questions to help your child develop reading comprehension and increase his/her awareness of words.

Approach this with a sense of play. Make a game of having your child answer the questions. You do not need to ask all the questions at one time. Let these questions be fun discussions rather than a test. If your child doesn't have instant recall, encourage him/her to look back into the book to "research" the answers. You'll be modeling what good readers do and, at the same time, forging a sharing bond with your child.

1. What magic word did Genie use?

2. How did Aladdin make the cookies disappear?

3. Why do genies learn to count to three?

4. Can you finish the alphabet game that the genies had started?

5. How many words can you find with the suffix -ed?

6. How many little words can you make from the letters in "Agrabah"?

Answers: 1. Ka-zam! 2. he ate them. 3. they can grant only three wishes. 4. A is for apple; B is for banana; C is for chocolate candy; D is for delicious; E is for erase; F is for float; G is for genie; H is for happy; etc. 5. *possible answers:* looked, grinned, finished, asked, replied, skipped, grabbed, laughed, rolled, added, snapped, appeared, popped, and disappeared. 6. *possible answers:* grab, bag, rag, bar, and gab.